Bill's Bike

by Andy Blackford

Illustrated by Hannah Wood

Crabtree Publishing Company
www.crabtreebooks.com

Crabtree Publishing Company

www.crabtreebooks.com

1-800-387-7650

616 Welland Ave.
St. Catharines, ON
L2M 5V6

PMB 59051, 350 Fifth Ave.
59th Floor,
New York, NY

Published by Crabtree Publishing in 2011

Series Editor: Jackie Hamley
Editor: Reagan Miller
Series Advisor: Catherine Glavina
Series Designer: Peter Scoulding
Project Coordinator: Kathy Middleton

Text © Andy Blackford 2010
Illustration © Hannah Wood 2010

Printed in Canada/122020/CPC20201213

First published in 2008
by Franklin Watts
(A division of Hachette
Children's Books)

The rights of the author and the illustrator of this Work have been asserted.

Library and Archives Canada Cataloguing in Publication

Blackford, Andy
    Bill's bike / by Andy Blackford ; illustrated by Hannah Wood.

(Tadpoles)
ISBN 978-0-7787-0575-8 (bound).--
ISBN 978-0-7787-0586-4 (pbk.)

    I. Wood, Hannah II. Title. III. Series: Tadpoles (St. Catharines, Ont.)

PZ7.B532Bi 2011   j823'.92   C2011-900150-0

Library of Congress Cataloging-in-Publication Data

Blackford, Andy.
 Bill's bike / by Andy Blackford ; illustrated by Hannah Wood.
     p. cm. -- (Tadpoles)
 Summary: Bill has a new bicycle with four wheels, but as he rides and rides he loses wheels one at a time until he finds out just how many he needs to have.
     ISBN 978-0-7787-0586-4 (pbk. : alk. paper) --
 ISBN 978-0-7787-0575-8 (reinforced library binding : alk. paper)
     [1. Bicycles and bicycling--Fiction. 2. Wheels--Fiction.]
 I. Wood, Hannah, ill. II. Title. III. Series.

PZ7.B53228Bil 2011
[E]--dc22
                                        2010052360

Here is a list of the words in this story.
Common words:

and	he	now
Dad	I	one
had	it	said

Other words:

bike	happy	three
Bill	need	two
birthday	only	wheels
four	rode	works

Bill's bike had four wheels.

5

Bill rode.

"I only need three wheels!" he said.

Bill rode and rode.

"I only need two wheels!" he said.

12

13

Bill rode and rode and rode.

"I only need one wheel!" he said.

"Help!" said Bill.

19

Puzzle Time

Can you find these
pictures in the story?

c

d

Which pages are the pictures from?

Answers

The pictures come from these pages:
a. pages 12 and 13
b. pages 18 and 19
c. pages 16 and 17
d. pages 6 and 7

Notes for adults

Tadpoles are structured to provide support for early readers. The stories may also be used by adults for sharing with young children.

Starting to read alone can be daunting. **Tadpoles** help by listing the words in the book for a preview before reading. **Tadpoles** also provide strong visual support and repeat words and phrases. These books will both develop confidence and encourage reading and rereading for pleasure.

If you are reading this book with a child, here are a few suggestions:

1. Make reading fun! Choose a time to read when you and the child are relaxed and have time to share the story.

2. Look at the picture on the front cover and read the blurb on the back cover. What might the story be about? Why might the child like it?

3. Look at the list of words on page two. Can the child identify most of the words?

4. Encourage the child to retell the story using the jumbled picture puzzle on pages 22-23.

5. Discuss the story and see if the child can relate it to his or her own experiences, or perhaps compare it to another story he or she knows.

6. Give praise! Children learn best in a positive environment.

If you enjoyed this book, why not try another **TADPOLES** story?
Please see the back cover for more **TADPOLES** titles.
Visit **www.crabtreebooks.com** for other **Crabtree** books.